P9-CEF-938

An IRVING & MUKTUK Story

DANIEL PINKWATER

ILLUSTRATED BY **JILL PINKWATER**

Houghton Mifflin Company
Boston 2005

For Bunny Boy

www.houghtonmifflinbooks.com

The text of this book is set in Leawood.
The illustrations were created with felt-tip marker and ink on Bristol board.

Library of Congress Cataloging-in-Publication Data
Pinkwater, Daniel Manus, 1941–
Bad bears and a bunny : an Irving and Muktuk story / by Daniel Pinkwater ; illustrated by Jill Pinkwater.
p. cm.
Summary: Although they intend to live up to their notorious reputations when they are invited to a fancy hotel party, polar bears Irving and Muktuk end up behaving themselves when a scary bunny shows up.
ISBN 0-618-33926-4
[1. Polar bear—Fiction. 2. Bears—Fiction. 3. Rabbits—Fiction. 4. Behavior—Fiction. 5. Humorous stories.] I. Pinkwater, Jill, ill. II. Title.
PZ7.P6335Bac 2005
[E]—dc22
2004013412

ISBN-13: 978-0618-33926-6

Manufactured in China
SCP 10 9 8 7 6 5 4 3 2 1

Irving and Muktuk are polar bears. They live in the zoo. They are not to be trusted. They are bad bears.

Whcn thcy livcd in thc frozcn North, thcy did many bad things until the people sent them away to the zoo in Bayonne, New Jersey. The bad things always involved stealing muffins.

There was another polar bear already at the zoo—Roy. Roy is quite a good bear. Roy lives in an apartment of his own and takes the bus to the zoo each morning.

ZOO

"Irving and Muktuk are bad bears, I have to say it," Roy tells the Director of the Zoo. "But they are not extremely bad. For example, they have never eaten a person—only muffins."

"It is good that they do not eat people," the Director of the Zoo says. "But they are bad bears, and not to be trusted."

One morning, a small white bunny appears. It is eating grass at the edge of the polar bear enclosure.

“Look at the tiny polar bear,” Irving says.
“I have never seen a polar bear that size,” Muktuk says.
“It looks dangerous,” Irving says.
“Let’s run inside and hide,” Muktuk says.

"That is not a polar bear," Roy says. "It is a bunny, an ordinary bunny."
"You're right! So it is! And not dangerous?" Irving and Muktuk ask.
"No."
"Let's tease it," Irving and Muktuk say.

"Hey, bunny-boy!" Irving and Muktuk shout. They waggle their ears and make rude bunny gestures.

"You . . . eat . . . grass! Grass-eater! Grass-eater! Yah, yah, yah!"

"Is that your nose, or are you eating a carrot?"

The bunny is fast. He runs at the bears. He kicks Irving in the ankle. He bites Muktuk on the toe. Then, he is back at the edge of the bear enclosure, eating grass as though nothing has happened.

"Owww! Owww! Did you see? The bunny attacked us!"
Irving and Muktuk run to their room.

Irving and Muktuk refuse to leave their room. Mr. Goldberg, the bear keeper, comes to see them. They are hiding under their blankets. Irving has put a bandage on his ankle, and Muktuk has put a bandage on his toe.

"The bunny is violent," Irving and Muktuk say. "Make him go away."

"This only happened because you teased him," Mr. Goldberg says.
"If you leave the bunny alone, he will leave you alone."
"No, he hates us!" the bears say. "He might eat us!"

"The bunny does not hate you, and he will not eat you," Mr. Goldberg says.
"He does! He will!" Irving and Muktuk say.
"I will speak to the bunny," Mr. Goldberg says.

Roy, the good polar bear, has a brother named Larry who is a lifeguard at a fancy hotel. He also lives at the hotel.

"Hey," Roy says to Irving and Muktuk. "If I invite you to a party, will you promise to behave?"

"A party?" Irving and Muktuk ask.

"At my brother Larry's," Roy says. "He says I can ask some of my friends. There is going to be blueberry muffin soup, and fishcakes."

"Your brother Larry who lives at the fancy hotel? Blueberry muffin soup? Fishcakes?"

"And ice cream."

"We can behave. Probably," Irving and Muktuk say.

"Okay," Roy says. "I'm going to trust you. No rough stuff, no stealing, no mocking or teasing, no making a mess."

"You know, we are not to be trusted," Irving and Muktuk say.

"I will take a chance. I think you will be good bears at this party."

When they are alone, Irving asks Muktuk, "Do you think we can behave ourselves at the party?"

"No," Muktuk answers.

"Well, Roy knew we weren't to be trusted," Irving says.

"Then it won't be our fault if we do bad things," Muktuk says.

Irving and Muktuk arrive at the party.

"What a fancy place!" Muktuk says.

"Look! The Zoo Director is here! And Mr. Goldberg! And there is Roy's brother Larry!" Irving says.

"And that is Mr. Frobisher, the owner of the hotel, and Mrs. Frobisher, and their daughter, little Mildred Frobisher," Muktuk says.

"And . . . oh! Oh! Look! No, don't look! Oh, no! It is . . . It is . . . the bunny!"

“The bunny is here?” Muktuk asks Irving.
“Don’t look.”

Irving whispers to Roy, “The bunny is here.”
“I know,” Roy says. “I invited him.”
“You invited him?” Muktuk asks.
“Yes,” Roy says. “He is a friend of mine.”
“Roy invited the bunny,” Muktuk whispers to Irving.
“Don’t look,” Irving whispers.

Irving and Muktuk sit as far from the bunny as they can. They take tiny bites of food and do not make noise, or break things, or try to steal things. They are careful not to look at the bunny.

"Is he watching us?" Irving asks Muktuk.

"I don't know," Muktuk whispers to Irving.

LIFEGUARD

When Mr. Frobisher invites the party guests to swim in the hotel pool, the bunny swims in the deep end and Irving and Muktuk stay in the shallow end.

"Don't splash," Muktuk whispers to Irving.

"Is he watching us?" Irving whispers to Muktuk.

"I don't know," Muktuk whispers.

After the party, Irving and Muktuk go back to the zoo.

"I didn't expect the bunny to be at the party," Muktuk says.

"I was nervous," Irving says. "I was afraid he was going to kick me in the ankle."

"Or bite me on the toe," Muktuk says. "But we did nothing to call attention to ourselves."

"We behaved perfectly," Irving says. "We were good bears the whole time we were there."